Hello, my Name is...

How Adorabilis Got His Name

To baby girl Polansky —M.P.

For my mom, Julia, who taught me not to be afraid of the ocean —J.C.

ISBN 978-1-338-30642-2

12 11 10 9 8 7 6 5 4 3 2 1   18 19 20 21 22 23

Printed in the U.S.A.   40

First Scholastic printing, September 2018

Designed by Kristie Radwilowicz

Hello, My Name is...

How Adorabilis Got His Name

Marisa Polansky

Pictures by Joey Chou

SCHOLASTIC INC.

Early one morning when all the fish were tucked away, a new creature arrived in the deep-sea tank. He was very tiny, with great big eyes and eight little tentacles. There had never been a creature quite like him.

"Good mooorning!"

said the friendly new creature. The other fish stirred with a start.

"Ooh, a new friend!" exclaimed **Yeti Crab.**

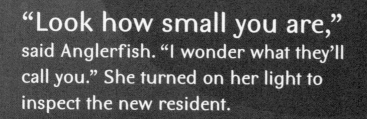

"Look how small you are,"
said Anglerfish. "I wonder what they'll
call you." She turned on her light to
inspect the new resident.

"Call me?" asked the
creature, looking confused.

"Well, everyone has a
name here. I use this
hook to attract fish like
an angler does, so I'm called
Anglerfish."

"I can change my shape and color, so I'm called **Mimic Octopus**," said an octopus the color of the coral behind her.

A fish smiled wide, showing his **long, sharp teeth**, and said, "I'm **Fangtooth**. Can you guess why?"

"And that's **Six-Gill Shark** because he has six gills he uses for breathing," said Anglerfish.

"Howdy, partner! What's your name?" said the shark, flipping his fin.

The new guy concentrated as hard as he could, but he couldn't change his color like Mimic Octopus.

He opened his mouth as wide as it would go, but he couldn't find one tooth.

He took a deep breath, but when he exhaled it was only out of two gills.

"What will my name be?"

"I can't do any of that either," said an orange-and-white striped fish. "But I have bright stripes like a painted clown, so they call me **Clown Fish.**"

"I glow bright white like the moon, so I'm known as **Moon Jelly,**" said a glamorous jellyfish as she stretched her tentacles.

"Wow," said the new creature. "You are all so incredible!"

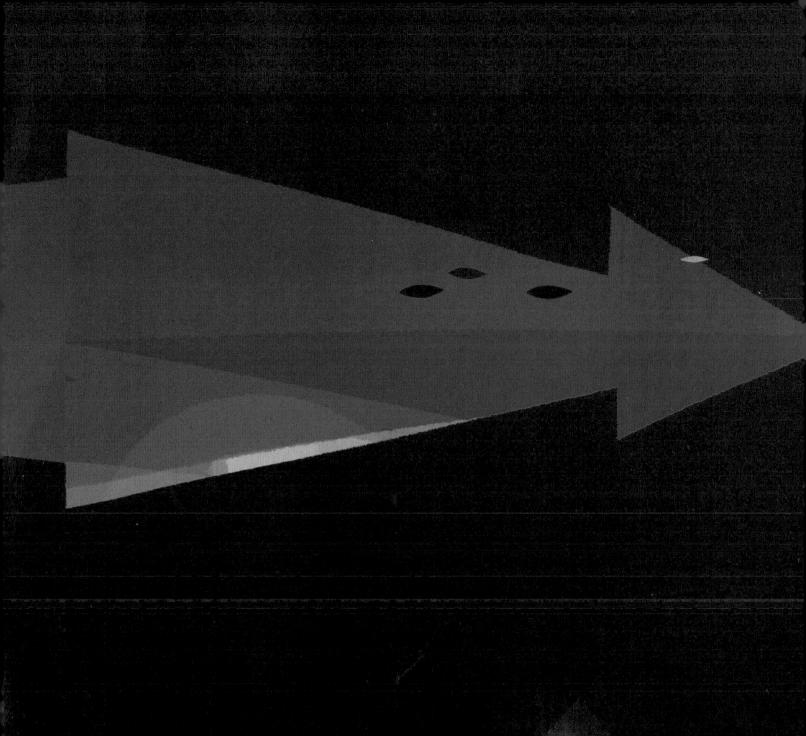

"That's **Giant Squid**. She's huge and powerful. I'd swim clear of her if I were you," whispered Anglerfish.

The new creature swam by the squid as quietly as he could.

As more fish gathered around,
the new guy grew more and
more uncertain about what his
name could be.

"I don't have bright stripes or look like the moon, and I'm definitely not giant.

"**What will I be called?**"

Just then,
he had an idea.

"Watch this!"
he said, jumping
off a high coral.

He gently floated
down to the bottom.
"I'm an excellent
parachute."

Then he wove in and out
of the sea plants.

"And I was the best
steerer in my old
neighborhood."

"They could call me
Parachute-Steerfish!"

"That's a mouthful,"
said Fangtooth with a big grin.

The new creature grew quiet.

What could his name possibly be?

Just then, a scientist appeared outside the tank. "How are you doing in your new home, Adorabilis?"

ADORABILIS

"Adorabilis!"

everyone exclaimed with excitement.

"You *are* adorable,"
said Clown Fish.

"Adorabilis is the
perfect name
for you," agreed
Anglerfish.

"I don't know. He looks
more like a Bob to me,"
said Six-Gill Shark.

"That's it! That's my name!" He tried it out.

"My name is ADOORA

BILIS!

Nice to meet you. "

A Note FROM A Scientist ON THE Naming OF Adorabilis

ADORABILIS IS A TYPE OF FLAPJACK OCTOPUS. This group of octopuses was given that name because they sometimes flatten themselves like pancakes on the bottom of the sea. This particular flapjack octopus has been found in deep water off the coast of California by scientists at the Monterey Bay Aquarium Research Institute using remotely operated vehicles (ROVs). ROVs are robots that use cameras and other instruments to explore parts of the ocean that are deeper than snorkelers and scuba divers can go. When some researchers captured a few of these small octopuses so people could see them at the Monterey Bay Aquarium, they realized the species needed an official name. Each animal and plant has two names that are used to describe it, like your first name and last name, but reversed, with the family name first. The first name was already known for this octopus. It is Opisthoteuthis. All of the octopuses with this first name are flapjack octopuses. So only the second name was needed. "Adorabilis" was suggested as a joke, because everyone agreed the little peach-pink octopus was very cute, and scientists started calling it that until they could decide on a more scientific second name. But before that happened, pictures and videos of this octopus species were posted on the Internet so people everywhere could see it. Lots of people thought that Adorabilis was the best last name to give this species.

Now that the name is chosen, scientists are working on learning more about this flapjack octopus. Adorabilis lives 700 to 3,000 feet deep, usually where the bottom is mostly mud. It is pretty dark and cold. The octopuses spend a large part of their time sitting on the bottom, looking for small worms and shrimps to eat. They crawl short distances over the bottom using their arms and webbing, but they are not fast, so when the water starts moving rapidly, they lift themselves off the bottom and steer through the water to a new place. There is still much to learn about this species, but it's certain that Adorabilis is adorable!

—Stephanie L. Bush, Monterey Bay Aquarium Research Institute

MARISA POLANSKY is a writer and editor. She is the author of the Today I'm A . . . board book series, as well as a founder of Speech Tank, a writing company specializing in one-of-a-kind speeches. She lives in Brooklyn, New York.

JOEY CHOU is an animator and illustrator. He has worked as a visual development artist on feature animated films and television, including *Kung Fu Panda: Legends of Awesomeness*. He is the illustrator of Disney's *Finding Nemo: Nemo's Day Off*, as well as *Ruby's Chinese New Year*, written by Vickie Lee. He lives in Los Angeles.